MW01109697

New Hampshire

by Patricia K. Kummer,
Capstone Press
Geography Department

Content Consultant:
William Copeley
Librarian
New Hampshire Historical Society

C A P S T O N E
H I G H / L O W B O O K S
an imprint of Capstone Press

C A P S T O N E   P R E S S

818 North Willow Street • Mankato, Minnesota 56001
http://www.capstone-press.com

Library of Congress Cataloging-in-Publication Data
Kummer, Patricia K.
    New Hampshire/by Patricia K. Kummer (Capstone Press, Geography Department).
          p. cm.--(One nation)
    Includes bibliographical references and index.
    Summary: An overview of the state of New Hampshire, including its history, geography, people, and living conditions.
    ISBN 1-56065-681-6
    1. New Hampshire--Juvenile literature. [1. New Hampshire.]
I. Capstone Press. Geography Dept. II. Title. III. Series.
F34.3.K86 1998
974.2--dc21
                                                                97-40819
                                                                CIP
                                                                AC

Editorial Credits: Editor, Cara Van Voorst; cover design and illustrations, Timothy Halldin; photo research, Michelle L. Norstad
Photo Credits:
Pat and Chuck Blackley, 29
Helen Longest Slaughter/Marty Saccone, 16, 20
Maguire Photografx/Joseph Maguire, 14, 40
Root Resources/Pat Wadecki, 6, 37
Lynn M. Stone, 10
Unicorn Stock Photos/Dick Keen, 5; Jean Higgins, 26; John Ward, 34
Visuals Unlimited/John Gerlach, cover; Barbara Gerlach, 4; Robert W. Domm, 5; John D. Cunningham, 9, 33; Mark E. Gibson, 23; Roger Treadwell, 30

Table of Contents

Fast Facts about New Hampshire

State Flag

Location: In the New England region of the northeastern United States

Size: 9,351 square miles (24,313 square kilometers)

Population: 1,162,481 (1996 U.S. Census Bureau estimate)

Capital: Concord

Date admitted to the Union: June 21, 1788; the ninth state

Purple finch

Purple lilac

Largest cities: Manchester, Nashua, Concord, Derry, Rochester, Portsmouth, Salem, Dover, Keene, Merrimack

Nickname: The Granite State

State animal: White-tailed deer

State bird: Purple finch

State flower: Purple lilac

State tree: White birch

State song: "Old New Hampshire" by John F. Holmes and Maurice Hoffman

White birch

Chapter 1

Government in the Granite State

Government is an important part of most New Hampshirites' lives. New Hampshirites have a big voice in choosing the president of the United States.

Since 1952, New Hampshire voters have chosen their favorite presidential candidates before voters in other states. New Hampshire holds its presidential primary election in early March. A presidential primary election is an election held in a state. Voters choose the candidates they would like to see in the final election. Other states hold their presidential primaries later in the year.

Government is an important part of most New Hampshirites' lives.

Importance of New Hampshire's Primary

New Hampshire holds its presidential primary every four years. Reporters and people in other states watch the results in New Hampshire. Candidates who do well in New Hampshire's primary usually do well across the nation.

Only one president since 1952 did not win in New Hampshire's primary. This happened in November 1992. Americans elected Bill Clinton president that year. Clinton had placed second in New Hampshire's primary.

Midnight at the Polls

New Hampshirites also cast the first votes for president in November. People in the tiny town of Dixville Notch begin voting just after midnight on election day. About 30 people vote. The results are announced across the nation.

In the past, the town of Hart's Location opened its polls at midnight. But townspeople grew tired of staying up late and talking to reporters. Hart's Location went back to regular voting hours for the 1968 election. In 1996, people in the town of Hart's Location decided to open their polls at midnight on election day again. They wanted their votes to receive as much attention as those of Dixville Notch's voters.

Town Meetings

The way New Hampshirites govern their towns is unusual. Once each year, towns across the state hold town meetings. Town meetings take place on the second Tuesday in March. New Hampshirites have held town meetings since the 1600s.

Townspeople elect town officials at the town meetings. The officials run town governments during the year. Townspeople also vote on local matters. For example, they might vote on whether to build a new school.

New Hampshirites cast the first votes for president in November.

Chapter 2

The Land

New Hampshire lies in the northeastern United States. It has a short coastline on the Atlantic Ocean. The state's lowest point is along this coastline. The coastline is at sea level. Sea level is the average level of the ocean's surface.

New Hampshire is one of the New England states. Three other New England states border New Hampshire. They are Massachusetts, Maine, and Vermont.

Quebec is New Hampshire's northern neighbor. This province is part of Canada. A province is a district or region within a country.

Granite forms most of New Hampshire's hills and mountains. That is why New Hampshire's nickname is the Granite State.

Granite forms most of New Hampshire's hills and mountains.

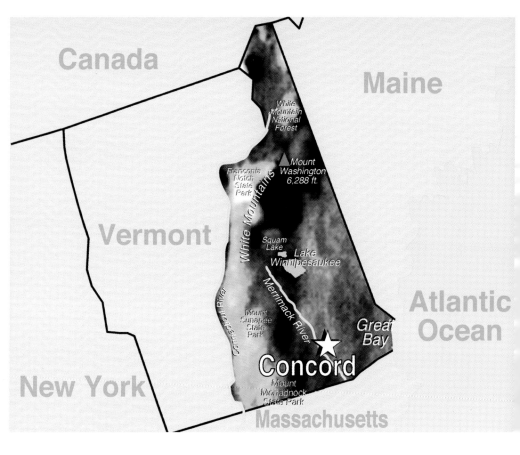

Coastal Lowlands

New Hampshire's Coastal Lowlands lie along the Atlantic Ocean. They extend about 20 miles (32 kilometers) from the coast.

Sandy beaches and saltwater marshes lie along the coast. A marsh is an area of low, wet land. Portsmouth is in the southern coastal region. This is New Hampshire's largest port.

The Isles of Shoals lie offshore. Four of these islands are part of New Hampshire. They are

Lunging, Seavey, Star, and White Islands. Five other islands belong to Maine.

New England Upland

The New England Upland covers the rest of southern New Hampshire. An upland is land that is higher than the land around it. Forests grow on much of the upland. Maple, ash, and oak trees grow in the forests.

The upland also contains large lakes. Winnipesaukee, Squam, and Sunapee are three upland lakes. Winnipesaukee is New Hampshire's largest lake.

The Merrimack Valley runs through the middle of the upland. This river valley has some of the state's largest granite quarries. A quarry is a place where stone is dug from the ground. New Hampshire's three largest cities are also in the valley. They are Manchester, Nashua, and Concord.

White Mountains Region

The White Mountains rise up in northern New Hampshire. These mountains are part of the Appalachian Mountains.

Mount Washington is New Hampshire's highest point.

Mount Washington is in the White Mountains. It is New Hampshire's highest point. Mount Washington's peak reaches 6,288 feet (1,917 meters) above sea level.

White Mountain National Forest stretches through the White Mountains. White pine and spruce trees grow there.

The Connecticut River

The Connecticut River starts in far northern New Hampshire. It forms the border between

New Hampshire and Vermont. The Connecticut River also flows through Massachusetts and Connecticut.

New Hampshire's richest farmland is in the Connecticut River Valley. Dairy cattle graze there. Vegetables and pine trees grow well in the valley's soil.

Wildlife

White-tailed deer and black bears live in New Hampshire's forests. Moose feed near its lakes. Ducks and geese nest around Great Bay. This bay is in southern New Hampshire.

Trout and bass swim in New Hampshire's rivers and lakes. Dolphins, seals, and whales live in the Atlantic Ocean off the New Hampshire coast.

Climate

New Hampshire has short, cool summers. Its winters are long, cold, and snowy. Northern New Hampshire receives more than 100 inches (254 centimeters) of snow each year.

The highest wind speed ever recorded was measured on Mount Washington. On April 12, 1934, wind blew across the mountain at 231 miles (372 kilometers) per hour.

Chapter 3
The People

Among the states, New Hampshire has the nation's ninth-smallest population. But the number of New Hampshirites continues to grow. Between 1980 and 1995, the state's population increased by more than 20 percent.

Most newcomers moved from other New England states. Many came from Massachusetts. Some of these people live in southern New Hampshire but still work in Massachusetts.

Where New Hampshirites Live

About half of the people in New Hampshire live in cities. Southern New Hampshire has the state's largest cities. Manchester, Nashua, and Concord

About half of the people in New Hampshire live in cities.

are in the Merrimack Valley. Rochester, Portsmouth, and Dover are in southeastern New Hampshire.

Fewer people live in northern New Hampshire. It is mostly mountains and forests.

Europeans

About 98 percent of New Hampshirites have European backgrounds. New Hampshire's early settlers were English or Scotch-Irish. Other Europeans came from Germany, Ireland, Poland, Greece, and Russia.

Beginning in the 1600s, many French people moved to Canada. Later, some of the French Canadians settled in New Hampshire. Most of the settlers worked in mills and lumber camps.

Canadian Americans

Almost 40 percent of New Hampshirites have some Canadian background. Hillsborough County has the fifth-highest population of Canadian Americans among U.S. counties.

Most of New Hampshire's Canadian Americans came from Quebec. This is Canada's French-speaking province. Many New

Hampshirites still speak French in their homes. Some New Hampshire radio stations feature programs in French.

African Americans

New Hampshire's first African Americans arrived in 1645. They were slaves. But few New Hampshirites ever owned slaves. By 1820, there were no slaves in the state.

Today, about 7,000 African Americans live in New Hampshire. African Americans make up less than one percent of New Hampshire's population.

Other Ethnic Groups

About 11,000 Hispanic Americans live in New Hampshire. Most of their families came from Puerto Rico or Mexico. Many have homes in Manchester, Nashua, or Portsmouth.

New Hampshire is home to about 9,000 Asian Americans. Many of their families came from China, India, or Korea. Most Asian Americans live in New Hampshire's large cities.

New Hampshire has the third-smallest population of Native Americans among U.S. states. About 2,100 Native Americans live there.

Chapter 4
New Hampshire History

People first arrived in present-day New Hampshire about 10,000 years ago. By the 1600s, about 5,000 Native Americans lived there. Most of them were Abenaki people. The Abenaki came from the region that is now Canada.

European Explorers

Europeans explored the coast of present-day New Hampshire during the early 1600s. They came back to England and France with stories

Early European explorers admired the forests of the New Hampshire area.

about the area. They gave reports about the area's fish, forests, and fur-bearing animals.

A British Colony
In the 1620s, British business people sent colonists to the area that is now New Hampshire. The business people wanted the colonists to send fish, lumber, and fur to Great Britain. The colonists built a town called Strawbery Banke where the city of Portsmouth now stands. They built another town in the area that is now Dover. They sent shiploads of goods to Great Britain.

The British ate the fish and made clothing from the fur. They made ship masts from the lumber. A mast is a tall pole that supports the sails of a boat or ship. People called New Hampshire's pine trees mast pines.

French and Indian Wars
Great Britain and France fought for control of North America during the late 1600s and early 1700s. Abenaki people from the New Hampshire

The early town of Strawbery Banke is now a museum.

area helped the French. Many others helped the British. These wars were the French and Indian Wars (1689-1763).

The Revolutionary War

The British won the French and Indian Wars. But these wars cost Great Britain a lot of money. Great Britain increased taxes on its 13 American colonies to help pay for the war. This angered the colonists.

The British and the colonists fought the Revolutionary War from 1775 to 1783. The American colonists fought for their independence from Great Britain. No battles took place in New Hampshire. However, hundreds of New Hampshirites fought the British army in other colonies.

In January 1776, New Hampshire formed a government separate from Great Britain. It was the first colony to do so.

The 13 colonies won the war in 1783. The colonies became a new country called the United States of America.

Textile mills opened in southern New Hampshire between 1800 and 1900.

The Constitution

Leaders of the new nation wanted a strong government. They wrote the U.S. Constitution. The Constitution contains the principles by which the United States is governed.

Nine states had to approve the Constitution before it became law. New Hampshire approved the Constitution in 1788. It was the ninth state to do so.

People built large hotels in New Hampshire's White Mountains.

Growth in New Hampshire

Between 1800 and 1900, New Hampshire gained almost 228,000 people. Many of them settled in the Merrimack and Connecticut River Valleys.

New Hampshire gained new businesses, too. The Portsmouth Naval Shipyard opened. Textile mills opened throughout southern New Hampshire. Textile is a kind of woven cloth. Mill

workers made yards of cotton and woolen cloth.
Shoe factories also opened.

Slavery and Civil War

Many New Hampshirites were abolitionists.
Abolitionists worked to end slavery in the United
States. Some New Hampshirites helped slaves
escape to Canada.

Slavery was a major cause of the Civil War
(1861-1865). Before that war, 11 Southern states
withdrew from the United States. The Southern
states formed a separate country called the
Confederate States of America. The Northern
states remained part of the Union.

People in Portsmouth built ships for the
Union. About 34,000 New Hampshirites helped
the Union win the war.

After the Civil War

New Hampshire's mills and factories grew larger
after the Civil War. Thousands of new workers
arrived. Most of these workers came from
Canada and Europe.

Tourism became a new business in New
Hampshire. People built large hotels in the White

Mountains. Visitors came to enjoy New Hampshire's nature areas.

World Wars and Depression

In 1917, the United States entered World War I (1914-1918). Workers in Portsmouth again built warships.

The Great Depression (1929-1939) hurt the entire country. The Great Depression was a period of national hardship. In New Hampshire, mills and factories closed. Many New Hampshirites lost their jobs.

In 1941, the United States entered World War II (1939-1945). Workers in New Hampshire's textile mills made cloth for soldiers' uniforms. People in shoe factories made boots. Workers in Portsmouth built submarines for the U.S. Navy.

Recent Challenges

Today, New Hampshire has few textile mills and shoe factories. Mill workers in southern states make more cloth than New Hampshirites. Workers in other countries make more shoes.

New Hampshire's government has worked to draw new businesses. Many computer companies have moved to the state.

Some visitors bike in New Hampshire's mountains.

Tourism has grown, too. Large resorts attract visitors to New Hampshire's mountains and lakeshores. Visitors hike, bike, ski, and swim there.

Today, New Hampshirites are working on a new problem. They are trying to keep growth from spoiling the state's environment. The environment is the natural world of land, water, and air.

Chapter 5

New Hampshire Business

In recent years, business has been good in New Hampshire. Workers' wages have increased. The state's unemployment rate is low. Less than four percent of New Hampshirites do not have jobs.

Manufacturing is New Hampshire's most important business. Service industries are also important. They include realty, tourism, and government work. Other important businesses include agriculture and mining.

Manufacturing

Computers are New Hampshire's leading manufactured product. The cities of Merrimack, Manchester, Nashua, and Portsmouth have large computer factories.

In recent years, business has been good in New Hampshire.

Scientific instruments are also important manufacured products. These products include tools used by doctors and scientists.

Manufacturers in southeastern New Hampshire make electronic equipment. Other manufacturers produce printed goods such as newspapers and magazines. Berlin is a town in northern New Hampshire. The town has a large paper mill.

Service Industries

Realty is a growing service business. Realty is the business of buying and selling land and buildings. In recent years, New Hampshire has gained more people and businesses. The newcomers have needed more homes and offices.

Tourism is another growing New Hampshire business. Each year, tourists spend about $4 billion in New Hampshire. Many visitors stay at ski resorts. Other people visit coastal or lakeside towns.

Many New Hampshirites work for the state or U.S. government. Some work at the Portsmouth Naval Shipyard. Some New Hampshirites work in state parks or national forests.

Dairy farming is New Hampshire's most important farm activity.

Agriculture and Mining

Dairy farming is New Hampshire's most important farm activity. Hay is New Hampshire's leading agricultural product. Potatoes and corn are the state's leading vegetables. Apples are the leading fruit. Maple syrup production is important on some New Hampshire farms.

Sand and gravel are New Hampshire's leading mining products. The largest supplies of sand and gravel are in south-central New Hampshire. Granite comes from a large quarry in Concord.

Chapter 6

Seeing the Sights

People in New Hampshire like to have fun. They enjoy more than 1,300 lakes during the summer. They fish, swim, and boat.

New Hampshire's colored fall leaves are famous for their beauty. Each winter, skiers race down the state's granite mountains. New Hampshire's seacoast and lakes also offer outdoor fun. Visitors learn about the state's history in cities and small towns.

The Seacoast

New Hampshire's oldest towns are near the seacoast. Dover was founded in 1623. It is New Hampshire's oldest town. The Woodman

New Hampshire's colored fall leaves are famous for their beauty.

Garrison House stands there. This museum has exhibits that show the area's history.

Portsmouth is south of Dover. This city started as Strawbery Banke in 1631. Today, Strawbery Banke is an outdoor museum. It has homes and shops from the 1600s.

Hampton Beach is south of Portsmouth. Visitors enjoy its white, sandy beach.

The Merrimack Valley

Concord is in the Merrimack Valley. Concord is the state capital. New Hampshire's capitol is made of New Hampshire granite.

Many visitors enjoy the Christa McAuliffe Planetarium. A planetarium is a building where visitors see images from space projected on a curved ceiling. Visitors can learn about space through hands-on exhibits.

Manchester is south of Concord. The Currier Gallery of Art is a famous art museum in Manchester.

Derry is southeast of Manchester. Robert Frost's home is in Derry. Robert Frost is a

New Hampshire's capitol is made of granite.

famous poet. He based many of his poems on his life in New Hampshire.

The Monadnock Region

The Monadnock Region covers southwestern New Hampshire. Several monadnocks rise above the land. A monadnock is a rocky mass that remains standing after land around it has worn down. Many people climb Mount Monadnock. It is 3,165 feet (965 meters) high.

Rindge is a town south of Mount Monadnock. An outdoor church called Cathedral of the Pines stands there. Visitors can see Mount Monadnock from the altar.

Keene is northwest of Mount Monadnock. Each October, Keene hosts the Pumpkin Festival. Townspeople have set world records by carving more than 10,000 pumpkins.

The Sunapee Region

Mount Sunapee State Park is north of Keene. New Hampshirites ski down Mount Sunapee during winter. During summer, people water-ski on Lake Sunapee. Each August, the park hosts the League of New Hampshire Craftsmen's Fair. This is the nation's oldest craft fair.

Hanover is northwest of Mount Sunapee State Park. Hanover is the home of Dartmouth College. Dartmouth is New Hampshire's oldest college. About 5,400 students attend classes at Dartmouth.

The Lakes Region

The Lakes Region is in central New Hampshire. Lake Winnipesaukee is in the middle of the region. This is New Hampshire's largest lake. Huge resorts and hotels line its shores.

Squam Lake is a lake north of Winnipesaukee. The Science Center of New Hampshire is near Squam Lake. Bobcats, bears, and deer live on the center's land. Researchers study wildlife there.

The White Mountains

The White Mountains rise above most of northern New Hampshire. More than 20 covered bridges cross rivers that flow through the mountains. Thousands of miles of ski trails mark the mountains' sides.

Jackson is in the eastern part of the White Mountains. Jackson is one of the world's best places for cross-country skiing. Skiers use more than 90 miles (145 kilometers) of trails.

The Presidential Range is west of Jackson. Its mountain peaks are named for U.S. presidents. The Mount Washington Cog Railway climbs up Mount Washington. It was the first railway in the nation built straight up a mountain. Workers built the railway in 1869.

Franconia Notch State Park is in the western part of the White Mountains. A notch is an opening between two mountains. The park includes a long gorge called the Flume. A gorge is a deep valley with steep, rocky sides. The Flume is 800 feet (244 meters) long. Water rushes between the Flume's granite walls.

The Old Man of the Mountain is a granite formation that looks like an old man's face.

The Old Man of the Mountain is also in the park. The Old Man of the Mountain is a granite formation. From special viewing points, five layers of granite look like an old man's face. This face is often used to represent the state of New Hampshire.

New Hampshire Time Line

About 8000 B.C.—People are living in the area that is now New Hampshire.

A.D. 1600—About 5,000 Native Americans are living in the area.

1614—English sea captain John Smith explores the New Hampshire area.

1623—Settlers found New Hampshire's first permanent non-Indian town, present-day Dover.

1629—John Mason names New Hampshire.

1679—England makes New Hampshire a colony.

1689-1763—New Hampshirites help England win the French and Indian Wars.

1770—Classes begin at Dartmouth College.

1775-1783—The 13 colonies fight and win the Revolutionary War.

1776—New Hampshire becomes the first colony to set up a government separate from Great Britain.

1788—New Hampshire becomes the ninth state.

1833—America's first public library is founded in Peterborough.

1853—Franklin Pierce of Hillsborough becomes the 14th president of the United States.

1934—The world's record wind speed of 231 miles (372 kilometers) per hour is recorded at Mount Washington.

1961—Alan B. Shepard Jr. of East Derry becomes the first American in space.

1963—New Hampshire starts the nation's first modern lottery to help pay for education.

1986—Concord high-school teacher Christa McAuliffe dies during the *Challenger* space shuttle explosion.

1990—New Hampshire's first nuclear power plant opens in Seabrook.

1996—New Hampshirites elect Jeanne Shaheen as the state's first female governor.

Famous
New Hampshirites

Mary Baker Eddy (1821-1910) Founder of the Christian Science Church, which teaches that prayer and knowing God can cure illness; born in Bow.

Mike Flanagan (1951-) Baseball player who pitched for the Baltimore Orioles and the Toronto Blue Jays; awarded the American League's Cy Young Award (1979); born in Manchester.

Robert Frost (1874-1963) Poet and teacher who won four Pulitzer Prizes in poetry (1924, 1931, 1937, 1943); moved to New Hampshire at age 10 and lived in Derry and Franconia.

Sarah Josepha Hale (1788-1879) Author and magazine editor; wrote "Mary Had a Little Lamb;" worked to make Thanksgiving a national holiday; born in Newport.

Kancamagus (1655?-1691?) Last chief of New Hampshire's Pennacook people; led his people to Canada after being defeated by colonists at the beginning of the French and Indian Wars.

Christa McAuliffe (1948-1986) High school teacher in Concord; died in the space shuttle *Challenger* explosion.

Franklin Pierce (1804-1869) Politician who became the only U.S. president from New Hampshire (1853-1857); born in Hillsborough.

Alan B. Shepard Jr. (1923-) Astronaut who became the first American in space (1961) and the fifth person to walk on the moon (1971); born in East Derry.

Daniel Webster (1782-1852) Speaker, Secretary of State, and U.S. Senator; born in Franklin.

Words to Know

abolitionist (ab-uh-LISH-uh-nist)—a person who works to outlaw slavery

monadnock (muh-NAD-nahk)—a rocky mass that remains standing after land around it has worn down

notch (NOCH)—an opening between two mountains

planetarium (plan-uh-TAIR-ee-uhm)—a building where visitors see images from space projected on a curved ceiling

textile (TEK-stile)—a kind of woven cloth

upland (UHP-land)—land that is higher than the surrounding land

To Learn More

Fradin, Dennis Brindell. *New Hampshire*. From Sea to Shining Sea. Chicago: Children's Press, 1992.

Thompson, Kathleen. *New Hampshire*. Portrait of America. Austin, Tex.: Raintree Steck-Vaughn, 1996.

Useful Addresses

Currier Gallery of Art
201 Myrtle Way
Manchester, NH 03104

Museum of New Hampshire History
Eagle Square
Concord, NH 03301

Strawbery Banke Museum
Marcy Street, P.O. Box 300
Portsmouth, NH 03802

Internet Sites

Excite Travel: New Hampshire, United States
http://city.net/countries/united_states/
   new_hampshire/
TRAVEL.org-NewHampshire.
http://travel.org/newhamp.html

Index